W9-BXU-461

104 E. Morgan
Tipton, MO 65081

Little
Red Riding Hood

Retold by Mabel W...

DATE DUE

Weste

© 1965 Weste... ...rved. Printed in the U.S.A. No part of this book may be ... ...an permission from the publisher. All trademarks are the property of Western Publishing Company, Inc. Library of Congress Catalog Card Number: 91-76047 ISBN: 0-307-00134-2   MCMXCIV

Many long summers ago, there was a little girl whose mother made her a red cape with a hood for her birthday.

Because it was so pretty, she wore it here, there, and everywhere. And that's why everyone called her Little Red Riding Hood.

One morning Mr. Whittle the woodcutter called at Little Red Riding Hood's cottage in the woods.

"Your grandmother is sick," he said, "and lonesome."

"May I take a basket of goodies to her?" Little Red Riding Hood asked her mother.

"That would cheer her up," Mother agreed. "It would make her feel better."

Mother put some cookies and butter rolls and fresh elderberry jam into a basket.

Little Red Riding Hood added a bag of colored jelly beans. Then she put on her red cape and kissed her mother good-bye.

"Keep to the path, child," said Mother. "Don't loiter along the way. And don't talk to strangers."

"I'll do just as you say, Mother," promised Little Red Riding Hood.

Then off she skipped, with the basket over her arm and her red cape flying in the breeze.

The birds sang merrily as Little Red Riding Hood walked through the shadowy woods. Bunnies hopped. Squirrels scampered. Fawns peeped shyly from among the trees.

"Good morning, friends," said Little Red Riding Hood.
"I'm sorry I can't stop to play with you today."
She pulled her hood onto her head and sang:
"Here I go to Grandma's house,
To Grandma's house I go!"

"Ho! Ho!" said a gruff, growly voice. "So *that's* where you're going!" And a great gray wolf pounced out from behind a blackberry bush.

"Please let me pass," said Little Red Riding Hood. "I must hurry!"

The wolf peeped into the basket. "Mm-mm," he said. "All my favorites!"

"All *Grandma's* favorites!" said Little Red Riding Hood. "Oh, please move aside."

"Wait a minute," said the wolf, becoming friendly. "Why not pick some flowers for your grandmother?"

"Well…" said Little Red Riding Hood, "I really shouldn't stop."

"A few minutes surely won't make any difference," said the wolf.

So Little Red Riding Hood stopped to pick some
bluebells and buttercups. By the time she had
gathered a pretty bouquet, the wolf was gone.

He was bounding along to Grandmother's house. "Here's the place," he said, and he knock-knock-knocked on the door.

"Who is there?" asked Grandmother.

"It's Little Red Riding Hood," called the wolf in a little-girl voice. "I've brought you a basket of goodies."

"Bless your heart!" said Grandmother. "Come in, dear!"

The wolf lifted the latch and laughed. "Boo!" he said.
Grandmother hopped out of bed and slipped
through the open door. *Zip!* she went through the
cabbage patch. *Zip!* through the woods.

After she had gone, the wicked wolf popped into one of Grandmother's nightgowns. Then he put on Grandmother's nightcap and spectacles and climbed into her bed.

Soon there was a knock on the door.
"Lift the latch, dear, and come in," called the wolf,
trying to sound like Grandmother.

Little Red Riding Hood hurried inside.

"Why, Grandma," she said, coming closer, "what long, furry ears you have!"

"All the better to hear you, my dear," said the wolf in a cheerful voice.

"And your eyes!" said Little Red Riding Hood. "Oh,
my! They look like big green marbles."
"All the better to see you, my dear!" said the wolf.

"My, oh my, Grandma," said Little Red Riding Hood, "what big white teeth you have!"

The wily, wicked wolf licked his chops. "All the better to EAT you!" he snapped, and he jumped out of bed.

But Little Red Riding Hood was quick. She skipped and hopped and circled around the room until the wolf was dizzy.

Then she ran through the door—straight into the arms of Mr. Whittle the woodcutter. "The wolf is after me!" cried Little Red Riding Hood.

"And we are after *him!*" added Grandmother, for she had brought the woodcutter to the cottage.

"You'll be sorry!" Mr. Whittle told the wolf. "Now it's *your* turn to be afraid."

The wolf yelped and ran for his life, with the woodcutter close behind.

"Everything's going to be all right now," Grandmother told Little Red Riding Hood.

And that's exactly how things turned out.

The woodcutter was soon back—all alone. "No more wolf," he said. "I don't think he'll ever stop running!"

"Hurray!" cried Little Red Riding Hood.

"Thank goodness!" said Grandmother.

    Then all three sat down to enjoy the goodies in Little
Red Riding Hood's basket—the cookies, the butter
rolls, the elderberry jam, and the jelly beans.
    The day was fine, after all.